I0452191

THE PRINCE HAS A BIG
SNAKE: The Rise & Fall of a Queen

by Nia Zola

from: *Africa Untold Tales*

ISBN: 978-1-967860-07-4

Paperback Version

Table of Contents

The Prince Has a Big Snake:

The Rise & Fall of a Queen

Queen Nyakara

In a vast African kingdom nestled between mountains and rivers, where lush forests meet the horizon, there lived a young queen whose beauty and intelligence were legendary. She was younger than most queens, but her wisdom exceeded her age. She had been born under the blue moon of Saturn when it coincided with Jupiter; she was a special child, and her parents knew it from her birth.

She was always meticulous about her diet and never ate junk food, so she grew up strong, healthy and filled out very nicely.

She was fastidious in school and made 100's and straight

A's on everything, in every subject. In her free time as a teen, she read everything she could find and was often found deep in thought.

But beneath her perfect image, a scandalous secret would develop in her life as a young adult. This secret could destroy everything she had worked for and built. This secret could derail and even take her life.

Prince Tumo

This is the story of a Prince who came and saw the beauty and splendors of Queen Nyakara. Although she was married when they met, he didn't care. Tumo was a lusty man with a big appetite for romance. He would woman watch from a balcony of his palace. He would sight passersby and then have them invited to the palace. Prince Tumo would often go to the market just to check out the local females. He was incorrigible, really.

Most of the wiser women avoided him when they'd see his entourage arrive, but the younger ones, the sillier ones still giggled and accepted his weak invitations. Too many of them dreamed of being his bride, since he was of age and single. But mysteriously none of the relationships with the local talent ever worked out.

Was it the snake? Was it just too big that it scared the women off? The prince has a snake, a big one, but we'll have to talk about that a bit later.

Tumo was dashing, handsome, charming, and rich. When he looked at women they melted, as if they melted right into him. This was some special charm that he carried that made the women swoon. So why didn't these relationships work out? Why didn't at least one of these connections turn into a royal marriage? Mostly, it was because Prince Tumo wanted to play around and not get a wife. His taste in women changed nearly every day so what would or could satisfy him? It wasn't just his taste in women that was diverse, it was his drive to conquer those women, to have relations with them as soon as possible, as often as possible, and without marriage.

He wanted this queen for himself, and he had been wanting her for a long time. Knowing the powers of his big snake, he was confident that he would get her. His charm and powers to seduce anyone and get whatever he wants is because of his big snake. There are whispers here and there about his snake, but few know for sure. Those who think they know are not sure and those who have ever seen it, refuse to speak of it. There were rumors that those who had seen that snake didn't even live to speak of it.

Prince Tumo, rich, and fine as hell, was spoiled, as princes can be sometimes. He was given everything from birth, but he wanted more. His parents tried to apportion out perks and gifts and money to him, but he wanted everything, and he wanted it right now. He lusted for things and stuff all day, every day.

One night a few years back, he wished upon a star that he happened to see fall from the sky and he had heard that if you make a wish on a falling star that it will come true.

Then, he went into his house and fell asleep. The next morning in the garden there was a baby snake; he brought it inside as his own pet. Tumo was not just an only child, he was also a lonely child. Soon, his pet snake began to grow so he found an area of the palace where no one ever went, and he hid it there. He'd go there daily to feed it and talk to it. One day he found out the snake could understand him and answer him. Posing as his friend, the Snake then made promises to Tumo if Tumo would do certain things for it.

The Snake lied and said, "I am your friend. Your good friend. Your best friend.

"Really," Tumo asked smiling? He felt he needed a friend.

"Tumo," it said, "if you do what I say I will get you everything you want."

"Everything?"

"Yes, everything and a lot of it, it you will just do as I say."

That day, the deal was struck.

King Jahlani

Queen Nyakara was born in a small village, the daughter of a humble healer. But even as a child, she had an aura of power that others could not ignore. Her sharp mind and unyielding determination set her apart from the other children. By the time she turned 18, she had outwitted and outmaneuvered many of the kingdom's most skilled advisors. She was among the brightest and the best and had gained the attention of the king.

One evening, King Jahlani, a man known for his wisdom and leadership called her to his palace. He saw potential in Nyakara and offered her a position as his closest advisor. Within a year, she had gained the king's trust and the loyalty of the people, becoming not just an advisor but the true power behind the throne.

The king proposed marriage and Nyakara, yearning for a father's attention, accepted marriage to this king who was old enough to be her father. King Jahlani had been born to the throne as was raised with the finest of everything. He wasn't a prideful man and since royalty was not new money to him or his family, he had an air of decorum that most didn't have. Put nicely, he was used to nice things and was not covetous or lustful.

He had been married but only two years prior he had lost his wife to a mysterious illness. She was a beloved queen. The people of the kingdom and her loyal and close palace servants and maidservants ministered to her to the end. She had come down with some strange illness which the people didn't know if it was from the water or if she had been attacked by a disease-carrying mosquito, or if it was something she ate. But one day she didn't feel well and then became weaker and weaker for about a month and then she never recovered.

The whole kingdom mourned and her closest maidservant, Asabe was beside herself with grief for months. She lost so much weight people started to wonder if she had contracted whatever disease the queen had and would waste away. But after about three months, her countenance brightened, and she was again able to take solid food, and she recovered completely. She had stated that she was devastated by the queen's death, and was sure to let the king know that she knew how he must be feeling and if ever, any time, for any reason, he needed anything that she would be available and would be by his side.

King Jahlani was gracious of her offer, but it didn't register with him as he preferred a butler or a manservant, but he was gracious enough to keep her on at the palace even though his wife had died. So, he saw her as a palace maid and nothing more. He then began to pour himself all the more into kingdom business to keep himself busy and keep his mind off of his loss and grief.

It was never a romantic plan when he invited Nyakara to the palace, but her beauty lifted his own countenance, and he enjoyed her sunny disposition, optimism and love for the people of the kingdom. He was as surprised as she was, so he proposed marriage to her.

Nyakara had hesitated, but her parents insisted and had said they wouldn't give their consent or blessings to any other man if she did not marry King Jahlani.

Therefore, she obeyed her parents.

The people adored her. The kingdom flourished under her guidance more than all the neighboring kingdoms. Because of the beautiful river that bordered the kingdom and the vast amounts of arable land and the willingness that the people had to work, they were able to produce many goods and send them to market on merchant ships. Thus, the kingdom flourished and prospered–, including all the people.

But as she rose higher in matters concerning the kingdom, the palace, and in the hearts of people, so did the whispers among some of the jealous ones.

How did she do it?

Some rudely suggested that she was a seductress. She most certainly was not. Some said she must have used charms on the king, after all her father is a healer. No, she did not use charms on the king.

King Jahlani had the option to have the high priest of the kingdom to prepare royal charms that would keep any other charms from working on him, but he didn't believe in all that stuff, so he didn't have any protective charms for his own sake or the palace. He believed in honesty and hard work and all things would just work out for the best.

In that kingdom, he would have to learn that he was very spiritually naïve.

So how did Nyakara do it? How did she win the heart of the widower king and also bring the kingdom up to a new level of prosperity, and so quickly? It was only two or three years that she had been queen.

Her answer: My father was a healer, so am I, but I am a different kind of healer. I seek peace and prosperity among people, and I believe we should follow the ancient laws to heal our land. People of a healed land are healed and healthy people.

Everything But...

In order for the queen to keep herself in that role she had to maintain all decorum and decency. That was no problem for her, she was raised in a good home, and she was pure when she married the king. Nyakara had never even had a boyfriend.

By now, with the accolades from the people of the kingdom and the approval of her husband, Queen Nyakara had everything she wanted: power, respect, and wealth. But there was one thing she lacked. Ironically, if she had not have gotten married, she never would have known that she lacked romance in her life. On their wedding night, Nyakara's first time, it was robotic, quick and then it was over with. Not only that, then her husband went to his own sleeping chambers and left her there alone.

Is this what marriage is about? She was disappointed. And that was sex? She was very disappointed. But romance was stimulated within her and she knew there was something more. Unfortunately, she could only daydream about it and wish she had a fiery husband with the kind of endurance that she could really enjoy.

So, what was missing for a queen who had it all?

Love. Two things if you add to love, attention. Her father was so caught up in his healing work, it was almost as though she didn't have a father.

Yes, she was queen because she had married the king of Nabiani, but he was married to the kingdom and always had been. She wondered why she didn't get time and attention from the men in her life? She felt as though the universe had conspired against her to keep her away from love and love away from her.

Instead of complaining, for most of her life, she had spent her time reading books and seeking knowledge anywhere she could.

Ever so often she tried to entice her husband, the King, but he was always, traveling, too busy, or too tired. If he gave her any time it was quick and unfulfilling, and then she'd still end up sleeping alone. This is royalty she asked herself? This is how they do it? Ugh!

Not having time for her, except for work and kingdom-related things, reminded her of her own father who was always too busy helping everyone else but her and the rest of the family.

To King Jahlani, her lawfully wedded husband, Nyakara, was for some reason downgraded to being a co-worker, someone to help him get things done and make him look good in meetings and at events. The people in the kingdom were prospering and the King gladly took credit for that and took all the glory; after all, he was the king.

Though he was a great leader, he was older, and their marriage had become more political than passionate. The king was not a fighter, but he wasn't a lover either--, at least not anymore. He had forgotten all about romance. He had forgotten all about the needs of a woman, especially a young woman. He didn't have the libido of a young man anymore, only a taste to rule and build the kingdom that was entrusted to him.

A Feast for the Eyes

One day, during a royal feast, Nyakara met Tumo, a young and charming prince from a neighboring kingdom. Their eyes locked, and an unspoken bond formed between them. But that eye lock didn't happen until Prince Tumo's eyes had locked in on her attributes.

For Nyakara what formed was a soul tie. The romantically inclined will believe that a soul tie is good, but it cannot be if she is already married to someone else and should not be tying her soul to anyone, least of all this hunk of a prince, Prince Tumo.

To Nyakara, not only was Prince Tumo everything her husband was not, he was also everything that she had been fantasizing about: he looked youthful, masculine, fiery, and passionate. She noticed him several times from across the room. She also noticed him noticing her. As well, Tumo noticed that he had her attention also. But, of course, Tumo knew he had this in the bag before he ever left home for this event.

Nyakara had never had a boyfriend and had never dated anyone when she came to the palace that night and met the king. But she did know what sex was and a strong sex drive had been awakened in her on her wedding night. She was feeling as though she had been starved of this kind of romantic attention in her dating years and even now, in her marriage. She had expected more, from the king--, a lot more, and a lot more often.

But she really didn't have a choice in husbands. By the time the king proposed to her, Nyakara's parents had insisted she marry the king. That was probably more for their own interest than hers. Her father set a very steep bride price which the king had no problem paying, so

Nyakara's family now because faux-royalty, I mean royalty by marriage.

Everything about Tumo had an air of mystery. At this royal feast, which turned out to be a feast for the eyes, once when the studly prince was walking past her, he seemed to have so much junk in the front that she couldn't tell if he was coming or going and that intrigued her even more. A little embarrassed, she quickly looked away, but as she scanned the room, she noticed that all the other women, young and old, royals, palace maids–, almost all the women were checking out Prince Tumo. She'd find out later that the women who didn't know his history and reputation with the ladies were the ones hoping for a chance to catch his attention.

What an allure he had.

At one point she realized that she may have lost control of herself or that she would lose control in the presence of this sex appeal, this allure, so she had excused herself from the gathering to try to avoid him. She wanted to avoid being obvious because she couldn't really take her eyes off of him and she didn't want to be disrespectful or be found out, either. She didn't know if she was imagining if he was constantly checking her out, but she felt that he was.

Nyakara knew she had to maintain decorum in public, and being a married woman, as young as she is, this couldn't or shouldn't go anywhere else. Furtive glances were the absolute most that could happen. She wondered how long her eyes stayed on him when they did land on his masculine build and virility; maybe people would notice. That is why she left the feast.

But within minutes her handmaiden, Asabe came up to get her, to see if she was okay--, and she was. And Asabe let her know that King Jahlani needed her at the banquet.

She obliged, of course. She was conflicted because she really wanted to go back, but she didn't want her desire for Prince Tumo to give her away.

Meet Prince Tumo

It was King Jahlani who formally introduced Nyakara to Prince Tumo with a hearty laugh stating that Tumo's dad and he had been long time friends and school classmates. And he remembers when Tumo was born and how proud his dad was to finally have a child, and a male heir, no less.

Oh, my goodness, thought Nyakara, this man really is old--, friends with this hot guy's dad. This is too much.

Nyakara put on a professional and royal face and said, "So nice to meet you."

"Likewise," said the young, studly prince as his eyes looked into hers like a laser.

The king explained to Nyakara that Prince Tumo had come to Nabiani to find out how the kingdom was prospering and maybe adopt some of their programs for his own kingdom. Well, that's what he told the King and Nyakara, that night.

Really, he had come under the guise of wanting to learn from them how their kingdom was prospering so that he could share that information back home and help his kingdom and his people. He said his kingdom was struggling and his people were suffering. That was true, however the palace, the royal family and Tumo, himself lacked for nothing.

The palace where Prince Tumo was born and raised was at least twice the size of the Palace of Nabiani. It had 3 living rooms, two kitchens, 12 bedrooms and several large, fine houses on the estate for long-term guests of the palace. It was either the pride or the bane of the existence of the impoverished people who lived in the kingdom as the royal family took all the proceeds that came into that kingdom for themselves and could not care at all about the commoners. They employed about 40 staff and servants to care for the estate, so how Tumo could ever say they needed help is beyond understanding and therefore what he said to Nyakara was a lie.

Actually, that was three lies, Tumo was a professional liar; he had learned from one of the best liars on Earth.

Queen Nyakara, who could normally see through the bull, was not paying attention as she should have been. Suddenly there is a specimen who is really her spec, and she has felt for years that she hasn't had any fun. Here's Tumo.

The prince had a reputation and the whispers were that he had a snake and that he could really please the ladies. Queen Nyakara had not heard any of those rumors, yet. But she was enthralled and seduced by his charm and good looks.

Tumo's lie made it possible for him to come to Nabiani once a month and for the Queen to travel to his kingdom to "help them out" also once a month. So, they began to see each other twice per month. First the meetings lasted one day, but then they decided that with all the travel involved they should make the meetings last two days, and then three. So eventually they saw one another six days a month, every month.

Did her husband, King Jahlani notice? Did he care? Well, he would have noticed, and he would have cared, but Tumo is the boy of his good lifelong friend, so what was there to worry about? When in Nabiani they were appropriate and respectful from what he could tell, and he didn't worry since his lifelong friend and his queen hosted Nyakara when she was in their kingdom.

Prince Tumo and Queen Nyakara both worked very well toward the same goal of convincing the queen that she was in love with this young stud, heartthrob and that he was in love with her.

When she went to his kingdom, there were no meetings at all, and she was okay with that. She met no one while she was there. Not only did she not meet the King or Queen, Tumo's parents, they didn't even know she was on the palace grounds. She was not entertained at the palace, but instead, a house near the palace where Prince Tumo lived. His parents were used to women coming and going and paid Tumo little attention. Plus, they knew their boy was a little weird and would often disappear for hours at a time. They were somewhat afraid of him.

It did not take long for their stolen moments to become filled with passion and desire. Prince Tumo wanted her to fall in love with him; actually, that was his goal. Tumo had come to Nabiani expressly to meet Nyakara, Queen Nyakara and to strike up a friendship with her, or even more --, a relationship. He came well prepared, well studied and equipped. Oh, he was fully equipped. His snake had helped him know what to do, what to say and he was filled out very nicely to attract and be attractive to the eyes of any hungry or thirsty soul at the royal feast.

The Dark Council

There is a council meeting of the Dark Council where they meet every 3rd and 5th day of each week. The evil council, which was in the spirit and not visible to the human eye was convened, met and held with the Snake at the head of the table, as the chair. The Snake is at the council room conference table; sometimes the snake takes the form of a man.

This particular meeting is about Nyakara, but it is not the first time they've met and discussed her. It is also not the first time they've met just to discuss her.

The dark side has been interested in her since she was born.

"She's a queen now, what do you think of that?" asked one of the attendees at the meeting.

"I don't think very much of that at all."

"They say her husband is a very wise man," chimed in another.

"That's nice--, he's wise, but he is not spiritual. He will do nothing to stop our efforts. Her husband, King Jahlani, spends so much time working that he is not spiritual at all. He doesn't even know that he, himself is being charmed and is under *our* spell to ignore his wife."

They all laughed in unison.

"Not only that, he hasn't *serviced* her but once or twice this year and she is starving for attention."

They laughed again as if on command.

"Not only that, but he has also been made to trust his friend, Tumo's father, so he has no worries that anything sexual could happen between Nyakara and Tumo."

The trap was set. They had been looking at Nyakara since her birth. She had a star that caught the star hunters' attention. It was the brightest of any in the village or the kingdom for the past 300 years. That meant there were talents, skills, abilities, promises from the Divine One, God in Heaven, whose name they hated to call and most often did not. They didn't want God, but they wanted what He had, and they wanted what He gave out to certain ones.

Nyakara was one of those certain ones. They spotted her star, and they wanted it.

Even though her father was a village healer and dabbled in the *arts* himself, in the name of healing people, he was so focused on the people who paid him, he gave little attention to his own family. He spent little time with his children. Nyakara was the eldest, but she wasn't a boy, she was just a girl, so her father basically ignored her, thinking she was not of much value to him except for receiving a bride price at some time in the future when he could marry her off to someone. And he did, to the richest man in the land, and he thanked his *gods* for that which he called good fortune.

Her father's lack of time for her growing up broke Nyakara's heart, so she worked very hard to excel in school and at everything she did, really to get her father's attention, but he didn't think that girls needed education at all and least of all not that much. Her dad was a little on the cheap side and resented paying her school fees, but he did it anyway at her mother's insistence.

Nyakara ended up getting the attention of the teachers at school, the principal and the community who celebrated her and that encouraged her to learn more, do more, be more.

She sat at the feet of any teacher and her capacity to learn and hold information and knowledge exceeded her age. Not only that, but she was also given the gift of Wisdom from God, even at birth and she was able to apply everything she learned to better herself, her family, and her community whenever she got the opportunity.

The Snake though, held an evil council meeting, because the snake was a principality.

The plan had always been and to continue to starve her of male attention, approval and affirmation so that she would either seek it out or she would be susceptible to it, or anything that looked like male attention, if it was offered to her. So it wasn't Nyakara's imagination that there was a conspiracy against her finding love, or receiving love, or having love.

The next part of the plan was to send in one of the Snake's operatives and drain her of every gift, skill, talent, virtue, ability and anything else that they could use, buy, sell or trade to any other lackluster sucker who came to the Snake to buy gifts that they didn't have and didn't deserve. This would also make Nyakara worthless, dimwitted, silly in life and no longer valuable. If possible, the Snake wanted to make her into an unstable vagabond. If she couldn't bring her gifts to the fore, those of the kingdom who would also benefit and be increased would remain poor, destitute and unsuccessful.

They would enjoy watching her fall.

Prince Tumo was the operative, he was the bait.

Nyakara's dad was so focused on money that he taught her very little about spiritual wickedness or spiritual things in general, so she fell right into the slow, long-term trap that was set for her years ago.

Suddenly, the Snake demanded, "Where's my cup? Where's my beverage? Where is Asabe?"

This reminded the Snake of the time that for 20 years or so Sadie brought him his cup, actually she had it on the table when the meeting started and didn't let it run dry, but one day she was just gone. He remembers asking for her and the other council members had stuttered, Uh, uh, the others present at the meeting had stammered and then explained that Sadie was no longer with them. The Snake asked, "What do you mean?" And then quickly decided that someone must bring his cup with his beverage because he was parched and he didn't really care who it was that brought it.

Guess Asabe was gone to. Easy come, easy go thought the Snake and went on with other topics at the meeting.

Meet My Snake

By the time the first night with Tumo had arrived, Nyakara had begun to hear the snake stories about him and found it amusing. She didn't think there could be anything wrong with a man with a big manhood. She was already nearly breathless with anticipation. She was a full blooded, hot-blooded young woman who had married an old man who didn't even come close to her expectations or needs.

That night she found out what the snake rumors were all about, Tumo was very well endowed and quite energetic. She was so enthralled with him that she didn't notice that in bed, his legs seem to disappear. No she had to be imagining that. The lights were out, there were a few candles, but she just knew what she felt, and it was powerful as far as she was concerned.

She chuckled to herself, but she was hooked. This man had charm and everything she wanted in a lover. Everything, and a lot of it.

Sometimes the man becomes the snake. The Snake is helping Prince Tumo to last and endure and get what he wants from Queen Nyakara so when the roles are flipped, the Snake can get the virtues of this young queen.

Nyakara and Tumo would have their fill of one another for three days straight when in his kingdom. She was so enchanted with his prowess that she didn't notice, as said before, sometimes the man *becomes* the Snake. She had absolutely no idea that Tumo was stealing from her or what he was stealing.

When Tumo came to Nabiani, it was a bit different. The prince did not board at the palace with the King and Queen, but was put in a guest house, and meetings with Nyakara were taken in the palace, so the King saw them appropriately sitting at a table in the meeting room discussing kingdom matters.

The king paid some attention, but not much, as he was handling affairs of state, while his wife was simply handling an affair.

But love is a dangerous thing in a world where power is everything.

She's Different Now

The kingdom began to notice that Queen Nyakara had become first distracted, and then distant. She was so distracted that she didn't notice that Tumo's kingdom wasn't poor and didn't look poor at all. As a matter of fact, it was opulent, so she concluded that he pretended that it was poor to get to her and with that explanation, she gave herself a compliment. Like a silly woman, she flattered herself.

But these days *she* was different. Queen Nyakara was getting less smart by the day; she was scatterbrained, almost an air brain. Her memory was shot, and she seemed distracted all the time.

The once unshakable confidence she displayed was gone; she was unsure of most things, or on some days she was unsure of everything. If you knew her before you would think she is not a confident person. If you didn't know her before you would almost swear that she was dense.

She was now clouded with guilt and anxiety. She kept rehearsing two things in her mind, memories of romance with Prince Tumo, and what if her husband found out. She was in deep thought about one of those two things all the time.

She was different these days, not as sharp. Not as happy. Not as friendly. She had no wisdom really to share with anyone. She became rather dull. Had she just lost interest in everything that used to hold her attention for hours and days?

Was she falling for Tumo? Oh, a new thought. And, then another--, she hoped she wasn't pregnant. Wonder what he's doing now. She would have spontaneous memories of their rendezvous and that would consume her mind for five and ten minutes at the time. She'd then have to get the person who was talking to repeat what they had just said.

Whispers of what is wrong with the Queen began to spread.

Queen Nyakara didn't notice that anything was different about her. She was too distracted an enthralled with the young Prince and let's face it, he was really *servicing* her with his "snake" and that is what she focused on.

Well, maybe she's a little bit more tired than usual, but she chalked that up to being a little bit more bored than usual, because with a firebrand like Prince Tumo, how was she supposed to focus on real life, if thoughts, fantasies and dreams of him were always occupying her mind? Her fatigue and ennui concerned her, she really hoped she wasn't pregnant, because if she was, she'd have to pin it on her husband, but how could she do that when they haven't slept in the same bed for months and months? Instead, she was giving to another man what belonged to her husband. And Tumo was gladly taking it. Not only that, he was taking what also belonged to Nyakara.

Turned It Down

Still, since she was an authority on growing the kingdom, word of her working with the kingdom next door began to travel and other kingdoms wanted to send delegations to take classes from Queen Nyakara as well.

She turned them down, she turned down the opportunity for growth and success and fulfillment for a man who wasn't even her husband, and as things stood, he could not ever be her husband.

She had thoughts going through her mind that never used to be there. She wondered what in the world could she possibly teach anyone. She wondered why people ever thought she was smart. Nyakara didn't realize that she must have bumped her head on the headboard too many times.

She turned down opportunity after opportunity to impart knowledge and help the neighboring kingdoms. She failed to realize that in doing so she would be helping her own kingdom. She knew it would take time away from Prince Tumo – and those other people couldn't sit in on her classes because she wasn't teaching any classes.

Tumo was holding class, with his big snake, that Nyakara felt was getting bigger each time she saw him. The queen was the student.

Kofi

As the affair continued, Nyakara's advisor, Kofi, a man she had known since childhood, who never should have been trusted to be an advisor kept his eyes on her. One would think that at his age he would be as a father figure to her, and he could have been. But, he was not. Kofi had always feigned loyalty to her, but he really was an opportunist. Kofi was a long-time friend and like a brother to Nyakara's father, so because her father trusted him so, Nyakara also did.

When he overheard a conversation between Nyakara and Tumo, he realized the truth. Wait! He thought to himself, she's the daughter of a herbalist, and she's married, and she has risen in life to become queen of this kingdom. Why is she seeing this young stud on the side and risking it all? She has morals and ethics to consider; she is a role model in this kingdom. Yet, she is seeing this young stud, this young prince– and he has a snake!

Kofi flashed back to his own life when he was 30 or so, 20 years ago. He fancied himself a ladies' man. He believed himself handsome and a real catch, so he chased women himself. Yet, here he was judging Tumo for doing the same. Then Kofi realized that he was sorry that those days had gone by him, and he couldn't do that anymore. Then he had to admit that he was jealous.

Kofi was a jealous man and even though admitting that he was jealous of a player Prince, he didn't admit to all of his jealousy. He was jealous that he wasn't royalty. He was jealous that he wasn't more important in the kingdom than he was. He was jealous that Nyakara, at her young age, was royalty, even coming from a humble background. He was jealous that Nyakara's parents, by her marriage to King Jahlani were now royalty. Kofi had chased so many women, he never had a wife or children, so no child of his could marry into royalty.

Prince Tumo had a snake. Seems everyone knew that Prince Tumo had a snake, except Queen Nyakara. Kofi pondered for a moment what it would have been like in his youth, or even now to have a snake. He mused that this may have made it possible for him to get everything he wanted from people. With a snake, he might be able to get everything he wants in life, and Kofi was a covetous man; he wanted everything. He wanted everything he saw and even things that he never saw but simply dreamed about.

The queen is having an affair. There is no way he would tell Nyakara's father, even though they were supposed to be close, like brothers. No, Kofi saw an opportunity to use the queen's secret to his advantage. Should he blackmail her for money, or go another route? He wouldn't dare approach Prince Tumo, he might end up arrested if he tried that on a man. What could he do, he wondered.

Kofi wanted to be the king's advisor, not just the advisor to a woman, even though she was a queen now. He sent a carefully crafted letter to the king, revealing the affair. The king was furious, his trust shattered, and he confronted Nyakara with the truth. It's as though this moment of finding out about the affair broke King Jahlani back to reality and out of the spell that he had been under. He didn't know he was under a spell, he had just been foggy headed, sleepy, not interested in sex, and overly focused on kingdom business. It never dawned on him that he wasn't and hadn't paid his wife much or any attention at all.

Of course, this affair was all her fault, how dare she! For a moment he thought about forgiving her and keeping her as his wife as long as no one else found out, but where had this letter come from?

Anonymous.

Who is that, and would they try to blackmail him? And who else would they tell? King Jahlani wanted to save face. He took a few days to think about this.

Meanwhile, Nyakara's perfect world was crashing down.

But that was not the worst of it. Kofi, seeing that the king's wrath could destroy Nyakara, decided to manipulate the situation further. He forged a letter, claiming that Nyakara had been plotting to overthrow the king, and presented it to the Council of Elders of the Kingdom of Nabiani.

The Council, already wary of Nyakara's power, especially over the king because they wanted the king's ear, and they also wanted to be his advisors. So, they took this evil letter and used it as an opportunity to demand that she be removed from the throne.

The king, first angry but then heartbroken and torn, had no choice but to obey. Nyakara was exiled from the palace, her name now tainted with scandal and betrayal.

All this because she was fascinated with Tumo's "snake".

Nyakara didn't know that she was surrounded by snakes. Looks like she had a snake too, her untrustworthy advisor-----, Kofi.

Kofi's Love Interest

Kofi, even at his age, had a love interest himself. She was Asabe, a stunning woman who seemed ageless. She was of a curvy build with all the right stuff in the right places. She had everything, and a lot of it. She had eyes and a smile that soothed Kofi whenever he saw her. Kofi was interested in her, but she wasn't interested in him. Asabe was interested in King Jahlani and had been for years. She too, was ambitious. Very ambitious.

Ever since the king had become a widower, she had tried to place herself in a position to get him to notice her as a woman. She was shocked and very hurt when he bought that, that child Nyakara into the palace and proposed to her. What was wrong with him, couldn't he see her? What was wrong with him? That small girl could be his daughter, nearly his granddaughter. What is wrong with men?

Asabe was a silently proactive woman. She had a charm on the King to be interested in her, but it didn't work, mainly because she put the love potion in some wine that the king did not drink, but instead, the King had given the wine to Kofi, which he graciously accepted with a broad grin on his face. Kofi drank it and the next moment Asabe came into the room, not knowing Kofi was there, thinking the King was alone. Kofi was love struck as soon as he saw Asabe. And as in days of his youth, he could feel his nature rising. That hadn't happened since forever, so he didn't fight it, he embraced it. He wanted to embrace Asabe if not right then and there, in private and soon and forever.

Asabe had already gotten a charm against the king and Nyakara having romantic relationship and had put it in the marriage chambers where Nyakara slept. This charm was also to keep Nyakara from getting pregnant by him. And, it was working, too. Asabe's sorcerer was powerful. But the love potion Asabe had prepared herself and, well it worked, but on the wrong man.

She was just so bothered by this Kofi always trying to talk to her or take her on a date. *Ewww*, he wasn't the King, so why was he bothering her, she wondered?

Expert in poison, how do you think the King got to be a widower?

Never drink wine with or from Asabe. Never eat any food she prepares or gives you; you've been warned.

Now You're Starless

If Nyakara ever knew that she had a star, she had completely forgotten it. In her star was her life, her success, her marriage, family, children, wealth, health, and prosperity. The stargazers employed by the Dark Council who had scoped out Nyakara's star when she was born knew that it was bright and if she maintained her star her future would be bright as well as everyone whose life she would touch.

She was supposed to teach multiple delegations of leaders from other kingdoms; this would have helped develop the part of the country where Nabiani sat.

Through a combination of foundational and parental issues, her father especially not paying attention to her and not teaching her spiritual things, her star became at risk at a very early age. The temptation to make money was orchestrated against her father while Nyakara was still a toddler, and he had fallen for it hook, line, and sinker. Of course, he did make money and that distracted him probably more than not making money. Either way, it was a curse and the Dark Council was pleased.

Thirdly, Nyakara was man starved, so Tumo or any man could have captured her through sex. The king, her husband could have, if they had had some energetic sex more than once or twice a year, on her birthday and his.

Her father was also guilty of not covering her spiritually. Her mother tried, but she wasn't very spiritual herself, so

Nyakara was just out there on her own, or at the mercy of the very limited knowledge of her schoolmates who didn't know very much about stars.

First her star was spotted. Then it was taken off course by a powerful wizard. Then it was covered, so by the time Tumo got to her, and she was so distracted by bedroom activities, the star hunters who worked for the dark council were able to completely steal her star. Some of them were traders in skills, gifts, abilities, virtues, stars and souls. They had collected quite a bit from Nyakara, so they felt their campaign was a success. While Nyakara didn't notice anything was being taken from her, until it was nearly all gone.

Forced Out

After being forced out of the palace, for **years**, Nyakara wandered through the villages, her heart heavy with regret. She had once been the most powerful woman in the kingdom, and now she was nothing but a shadow of her former self. She couldn't seem to pull herself together again.

She didn't want to be a divorcee and ruined in life, so after some months of frustration and loneliness, one night she went to Tumo's guest house, the one she always stayed in and waited for him, and his snake there. When he came in he was not happy to see her. He yelled at her as if she were a stranger who had squatted in his property. She tried to seduce him, but he sent her away but let her stay in another remote guest house on the property. What little sleep she could get; she got it there. Tumo had forcefully insisted that she must leave by daybreak the next morning so his parents, the king and queen of that kingdom would not see her. He reminded her that his father and King Jahlani were long-time friends.

Nyakara was absolutely humiliated when Tumo had said, "I can't stand the sight of you, the smell of you. I don't even know what I ever saw in you in the first place."

Nyakara was horrified and so hurt. She had cried most of the night until she was completely exhausted. She had slept, but very little.

The prince didn't want to see her again--, not ever, he had said. That hurt Nyakara badly though because it was as though he suddenly hated her and was disgusted by her very presence. Still, she rationalized, there'd be nothing but scandals and more scandals. Part of her wanted to be with him or still wanted to be with him, but how could his parents ever accept the sordid wife of the prince's father's schoolmate friend?

Tumo did not want to see her after the scandal, how could he even if he wanted to?

After some years, Kofi who was an old man and had died mysteriously. It was said that he had died of a heart attack. Nyakara hadn't held a grudge against him anyway, since she supposed the truth had to come out some way or other, as bad as it hurt and had ruined her life. She never knew though that he was the one telling the elders that she wanted to take over the kingdom.

The Dark Council was laughing hysterically. They hadn't even counted on Kofi helping them. But still they felt very successful.

Sacrifice

Prince Tumo, in the secret rooms in a wing of the palace where no one really went stands talking to his snake. The snake is huge and sits erect like a person. It can take on different sizes, but today it wasn't to be menacing to Tumo so today it is taller than three Tumo's and is very full of himself. As said, he is a whole principality.

If only Queen Nyakara could see Prince Tumo really does have a snake, and it talks with him, advises him, tells him what to do, and Prince Tumo does it.

If Queen Nyakara could see how Prince Tumo's kingdom had grown from the time that Tumo got that snake as a baby snake in the garden and brought it into the house as a pet. Tumo's kingdom was already rich because Tumo worshipped that snake, but the kingdom had gotten richer since Tumo had met and started sleeping with Nyakara.

Tumo's kingdom had gotten even richer suddenly both his mother and father had died and now he was King Tumo—a king with no queen and no prospects of a queen.

If only Nyakara or anyone who was listening or interested could see hos Tumo's kingdom had grown every time he got a girlfriend and began to sleep with her, no matter who that girlfriend was. They would have been astonished, even in disbelief, to see how every time an ex-girlfriend went missing the kingdom grew. Had they known there was a secret graveyard back behind the palace where only Tumo and the Snake knew about. The girlfriends didn't just go missing, move away, or run away although that was how Tumo explained the loss of another potential bride. No, it was Tumo and the Snake partners in crime.

Had people known, they could have put a stop to all this bloodshed, and all this loss and mourning in the kingdom.

That Dark Night

That dark night that Nyakara had risked so much and went to the palace at Tumo's estate and waited for him was the worst night that she could possibly have thought of doing such. That was the night the Snake was demanding blood; he was demanding sacrifice and Tumo had only until midnight to provide what he wanted, or the Snake said he would take blood where he would take blood.

Somehow the Snake knew that Nyakara was coming to the kingdom to see Tumo. It had been discussed in the Dark Council meeting. They had been working on her, urging her, coaxing her and dropping ideas into her head. They had been giving her instructions in her dream, *Go see Tumo.*

Nyakara did not hear these suggestions with her own ears but felt them inside of her and thought these were her own ideas. *Go see Tumo. He will marry you. Go see Tumo, he will accept you. Go see Tumo, you and he can rule that kingdom together. Tumo's parents are old, you and Tumo can be king and queen there as a couple. Go see Tumo.*

They knew she would be coming to Tumo because they had instructed her to do so and after a certain time, she complied with their evil wishes, which were all lies and not true at all.

They did all this because the Snake, who had stripped Nyakara of all her virtues and redeeming qualities, now wanted her blood.

Prince Tumo, even though he was a womanizer, was more valiant than we give him credit for. He knew the Snake wanted Nyakara's blood because that is the pattern the snake had followed all of his dating life since he had met that reptile. Tumo was purposefully staying away from Nyakara to protect her, to save her life.

That dark night was the night that the Snake would strike, so Tumo took her and hid her in another house altogether where the Snake would never guess she would be. And then he ran her off at dawn the next morning with all kinds of excuses as to why she must go.

Tumo loved Nyakara, but he told her the very opposite. His actions though proved it.

The Snake was not one to be toyed with. He knew Nyakara was in the palace compound but was not able to find her for some reason. After about 3am he was very angry and those who monitor for him had failed and were tired of looking for her.

Figuring she was in bed with Tumo, they were searching for two people in a bedroom. They tricked the Snake and said, The one you are looking for are in the king and the queen's chambers. They are trying to trick you, they lied without shame to the monitoring spirits.

The Snake sent spiritual assassins out to kill the woman and the man. They killed the King and Queen, Tumo's parents in their sleep and they never woke up again. While all this was going on, Nyakara was slipping out of the gates of the palace, past the same palace guards that she had bribed to get into the palace grounds in the first place, only this time they were sound asleep.

If Only She Could See

All the women Tumo was interested in were dying, everyone except Nyakara. They died mysterious deaths. They died of sudden fevers, heart issues, head problems, spontaneous bleeding --, you name it. More than one was reported missing or said to have run away and were never heard from again.

So now he is king -- King Tumo with a snake. No wife. But a snake that he does things to.

The snake begins to speak and says, "The sacrifices were accepted this time. Next time I will ask for more"

Shocked, King Tumo says, "Next time! What next time? You never used to ask for blood like that. Never two at a time, it was always one per year. Plus, you're getting too big."

There was no pause as the snake was sharp tongued, "Things change. And you like getting big, don't you? You like wealth, don't you? Well, I like sacrifices."

But, but, those were my parents.

Drily the snake responds, "And?" Then there was a short pause and the Snake continues: I made it look like an accident.

Well, I guess you had to, it's not the like King and Queen of the kingdom ran away to another kingdom or to the city and just abdicated the throne.

That's true, but no one suspects a thing.

Maybe we want them to suspect a thing, Snake.

If they did, Tumo, they'd suspect you and never me. I don't exist, remember?

Tumo knew that line of conversation would not go in his favor, so he went back to the previous conversation: You told me once I drained the queen of her virtues that everything would be settled, and we'd be done.

We are never done, TUMO--. NEVER! NEVER! Tumo, it called as the defeated man was leaving the room. You're king now.

Yes. So?

King requires a different level of sacrifice than just being a prince, so hop to it.

Hop to what?

What you're deaf? You didn't hear me? You'd better find another queen to drain; we've made a lot of money off of her brainpower and her talents, and virtues. If you don't soon find another – *you'll* be next.

Tumo gasps, looks in shock, astonishment, and extreme fear, then hangs his head in defeat. At least, he thought to himself, I have saved Nyakara. Then he sighed to himself as he left the room, Nyakara, I am so sorry. I have not just ruined your life; I almost caused you to lose it. I'm so sorry.

Prosperity Lost

After Queen Nyakara was removed from the throne and the palace, suddenly the prosperity of the kingdom began to change. Crops in Nabiani wouldn't grow. People couldn't find jobs. The craftsmen of the village couldn't sell their wares where they used to be so popular.

Even the river dried up ½ the year and trade stopped from the kingdom of Nabiani, and people became poor and disheartened.

The villagers, remembering her as the great queen who had brought prosperity to their land, were divided. Some blamed her for her betrayal, while others believed she had been unjustly cast aside.

Others believed that God was punishing her and them for her infidelity. They assumed the same devastation was happening to Tumo, although they didn't know that he was prospering beyond his wildest dreams and living his best life, over in his kingdom.

Silver and gold and goods, and money was flowing in from every source, but the people were unhappy, even miserable. They felt oppressed, with a feeling of doom, but they had money. People without money think that money is what they need to be happy. The people of Tumo's kingdom started to have money, but they were conflicted, and it was a weird feeling for them, and they didn't know why. It's like the rich people who are unhappy or bored but they don't understand it, since they have all material goods and everything they need financially. They are just not happy or fulfilled. Something is still missing.

Because of King Tumo's façade the commoners would never suspect that their prosperity was ill-gotten. Money gotten decently and properly will bless people and make them very happy, while ill-gotten gains have sorrow with it.

Sage's Lady

One day, Nyakara sat by the edge of a river, reflecting on her fall from grace, as she had done countless times since being removed from the palace. It was as though she was a vagabond, wandering all day without doing anything of purpose or real value. She had stopped accomplishing anything and had become a shadow of herself. This particular day an older woman approached her. This woman was known for her wisdom and had helped heal many who came seeking solace. She introduced herself as Sadie, and asked Nyakara why she looked so broken.

"I lost everything," Nyakara replied, her voice filled with sorrow. "I was betrayed, and I betrayed those who trusted me. I was consumed with lust, and in the end, it destroyed me." Nyakara didn't even know why she was speaking so freely and telling this woman her life's story, or why this woman would even care.

The old woman smiled softly. "You are not the first to be tempted by the pleasures of the flesh, nor will you be the last.   But, while you were in your temptation, you were attacked."

Nyakara's head snapped around as she asked, "Attacked! How so?"

"Yes, attacked my queen. You were attacked spiritually by a man who came to drain your virtues."

"Me? Was it Kofi?" Nyakara said while silently thinking no one has called her my Queen for years. Who was this woman?

"Yes you, but it was not Kofi."

"But who?"

"Tumo."

"Tumo?"

"Yes, you know he has a snake."

"Why people keep talking about that man's private parts is confusing to Nyakara. You even know about his --- --- she stutters --- down there?"

The woman laughs, "I'm not talking about his private parts, I am talking about his snake. He has a real snake; they say it is a very big snake."

Nyakara shyly asks, "What do you mean?"

"My queen, Isn't your father a herbalist? She pauses for a moment then continues, "Don't you know about the ritual snake? Didn't your father teach you about spiritual things?"

"No. I didn't know anything of what my father did. My mother insisted that I concentrate on schoolwork and studying so I would make good grades. "

"Oh, I see. Well, your soul was thirsty and then captured by that charming young man. His purpose was to drain you of every good gift, talent, skill and ability that the good Lord gave you. While you were distracted getting yourself entangled with him every other weekend or so, he was draining you and feeding your gifts to the snake.

The snake in turn used your natural gifts to prosper Tumo and his own kingdom while draining yours."

Queen: why did he pick me. You are a very gifted woman; the dark kingdom has been eyeing you since the day you were born. I know, because I used to be on the dark side, now I'm not. They stole the prosperity of Nabiani and gave it to Tumo's kingdom as a reward for all the evil he did for the Snake.

Evil? What evil?

Oh, my Queen, it started a long time ago. Prince Tumo is not what he seems to be.

Queen Nyakara asks, How was he doing that? Why was he doing that?

Sadie GLARES at Nyakara. How do you think? The same thing he was doing to you, he was then doing to the snake.

Why?

Greed. Lust for power.

Nyakara exclaims, "What! Why? That's disgusting! Nyakara suddenly felt a wave of hatred for Tumo and suddenly threw up.

The wise woman continues, just like you just did, "The snake would vomit up Gold. Right there on the spot. The more he did you, the more gold he would vomit and spit out."

That is the gist of your problems; it is the reason you are out of the palace and displaced from your marriage.

Miss Sadie, I'm not guilt free, I did things that I shouldn't have done myself.

Do you know a woman named Asabe is she still at the palace?

Yes. She was my handmaiden. How do you know her?

"I know her from long ago. We used to go to the same dark council meetings--, we were in training and servants back then. I left, but she stayed. Anyway, she put a beauty curse on you to make you unattractive to the king."

"King Jahlani! My husband?"

And to keep you from getting pregnant."

What! What? What did you just say?

To keep you from getting pregnant."

"So, that's why--, Nyakara said, so many times I was worried that I would get pregnant for Tumo--."

"There was a spell on you to not get pregnant for anyone, my Queen.

"And as for King Jahlani, that's why he was always busy and traveling and had so many excuses. Until you were married, he was very attracted to you, but Asabe put a spell on him that after your first night he would lose interest not just in you, but in sex altogether except for with one person."

"Who?"

"My Queen--, herself. She was interested in King Jahlani for herself."

"But she was his wife's handmaiden. And then she stayed on at the palace and became mine--," Nyakara became very silent and began to put some things together. Then she dared ask, "Is that what happened to the queen before me?"

"Yes, and it was going to happen to you too, Asabe stops at nothing, she is full of evil. But you were away from the palace so much that she couldn't exact her plan against you."

"How, how did she do it--, I mean to the queen?"

"Poison."

Nyakara's eyes grew large, and her neck craned as if that would make her hear better. "Asabe did this?"

"Yes, Asabe. She put a little bit of poison in King Jahlani's wife's food every day so she wouldn't die suddenly, but a little at a time. She did all this evil while being her maidservant and smiling in her face every day. She had convinced the queen to only trust her because the cooks and the other servants were suspicious."

"My God! Who else knows this? Is she in prison?"

"We will get to her, but for now let's focus on you and why you sit here day after day, all alone, staring at the river."

Nyakara was sobering up and coming back to her senses. Her pause caused Sadie to pause, then the wise woman continued. "And then she tried to extend the beauty curse to make you unattractive to Prince Tumo."

"Why? She didn't want me to cheat on King Jahlani?" Nyakara asked and then answered with her own theory. "Well, that may have been a good thing, I needed to stop sleeping with Tumo."

"Well, what the devil means for harm."

Wait--, is this why he suddenly didn't want to see me anymore? The curse against your beauty so that Tumo would not be attracted to you because she was jealous of you.

"Jealous of me? But why, she's a whole grown woman. I'm basically a small girl?"

"King Jahlani."

"What? How do you know all this?"

"I used to be on the dark side, my Queen, so I can see darkness. I can sense it; I can almost smell it.

"Asabe was good with poisons but not with beauty spells. So, her spells against you didn't work on Tumo because the charms he was using were greater than the charms she was using."

"So, what happened?"

"A war in the spirit."

"A war?"

"Yes, and the *gods* she was praying to were sat down by the *gods* that Tumo was working with. In order for the spell to work against you means that it would have to also work against Tumo. Her lesser *gods* couldn't get past the Snake. Even though the Snake had Tumo doing evil, the Snake still protected Tumo in the spirit because if anything happened to Tumo it would mess up the Snake's plans."

"Oh my! That's complicated," exclaimed Nyakara. "So, what happened, she asked again?"

Asabe's spells all backfired on her and she suddenly became shriveled up and old and wrinkled far before her time. All the beauty she had exchanged and stolen from others was removed from her.

"Where is she now?"

"She is dead."

"Dead? What happened to her?"

"That last night for her and Kofi, he finally got her to come into his bedroom and he was all over her the way it was told by those in the hallway who heard them. They said it was very loud in there. It seems they were in the throes of passion--."

"Kofi!" exclaimed Nyakara; the thought was almost too much for her.

"Kofi," asserted Sadie with a firm look at Nyakara. "They were in the heat of the moment when Kofi opened his eyes and saw that he was with an old hag and not the beautiful Asabe that he had been fantasizing about for months. He got up from the bed and beat her to death out of fear. He thought he was having relations with a ghost or a spirit. The people said the door was locked but they could hear him praying with each thump and thud of his fist on flesh. They said he sounded like a mad, praying silverback gorilla."

"Oh!" gasped Nyakara.

"Then they said it was suddenly quiet in that room, then Kofi cried out in agonizing pain and died. When it was all quiet in there, they broke the door down and saw Kofi lying there clutching his heart. It must have been a heart attack.

"On his desk was the letter he had written absolving you from any wrongdoing as it concerned taking over the kingdom."

"I never wanted to take over the kingdom. I never even wanted to marry the king, but my parents made me."

"I know, my Queen. I know."

The Snake Must Die

Nyakara puts her head into her hands and moans, "Oh, I was such a fool." Then she frantically asks, "What can I do? How can I fix this?" The she says slowly, in disbelief, "Can I even fix this?"

"Well, you've stopped the behavior, some years ago; that's a start. Next you have to repent and never do it again. Pray for your virtues, skills, gifts, natural talents, abilities and blessings back. You've got to get them back from Tumo and the Snake, and whomever is enjoying your blessings. "

"I'll do it! And--, Nyakara is almost afraid to ask… "what about the Snake."

"It must die!" the wise woman proclaims!

"How?"

"When you pray and repent and renounce your behavior it will strike fear and death on the snake, automatically."

Nyakara listened carefully, and for the first time in years, she felt a flicker of hope. She began praying and repenting of every sin she knew of and could think of. After some days of consistent prayer, she began to look pretty again—the Snake had drained her beauty. Now her prayers were draining it back. The power Nyakara was praying to was greater than any of the gods that Asabe or Tumo had invoked. That power is far greater than the power that the Snake used.

Day by day, and also through many nights she prayed and prayed. She hadn't prayed for years and felt like the dryness in her soul was being watered and her thirst was being quenched. She hadn't prayed to this God, the real God because her father had played around with so many lesser spirits that he forbade his family to call on the real God of Heaven and Earth because he thought the real God of the Universe would smite him. Now, this God of Heaven and Earth was Nyakara's only hope.

It's Not Big Anymore

King Tumo noticed his large coiling snake was wrinkling and drying up and getting weaker and weaker and he didn't know why. It stopped talking; it didn't speak anymore. It didn't vomit out any more gold either --, well, it was not as if King Tumo needed any more gold anyway. So Tumo hadn't been feeding the Snake either, even though the Snake was demanding it. Tumo was so angry about the loss of his parents that he barely even went to the Snake anymore, but the Snake said if you don't come here, I will come out of this room and I will go where you are, and follow you everywhere, then everyone will know the source of your powers.

Tumo wanted to represent to his subjects that he was good and a decent and

God-fearing man. There is no way he wanted them to see the Snake even though rumors had swirled about his kingdom for years. Rumors had gone around that the Snake had even killed his parents and that's why he was now king.

Tumo was conflicted because he knew the Snake would ask for another sacrifice soon and he didn't have anyone that he could sacrifice, except some of the commoners in his kingdom–, but which one? Which one would the snake approve of? As the snake got weaker, Tumo became more hopeful that maybe that snake would die. He regretted having made the deal with the snake in the first place.

Maybe it would die, Tumo hoped, or prayed.

One day Tumo entered the secret room where the Snake lived, and it was not moving. It seemed in deep sleep, or completely lifeless. Tumo wanted to rejoice, but he didn't know if the Snake was faking or not. He wanted to touch it, but he didn't. He had already touched that Snake more times than he cared to remember. And, anyway, how wouldn't he know if a cold snake was dead or not? It was always cold.

He couldn't resist, he had to know. Tumo reached out his hand and touched the reptile, and at that exact moment lightning shot from the ceiling and the wall from the Snake to Tumo. King Tumo dropped dead, and the Snake disintegrated as if it had never been there.

When evil is deeply embedded sometimes the man becomes the Snake and sometimes the Snake becomes the man.

Beauty Restored

Nyakara: became young and beautiful again, as if she was 10 years younger than she had looked for the past few years.

With a new courage, she returned to the palace, not to reclaim her throne, but to face those she had wronged. She asked the king for forgiveness, acknowledging her mistakes and vowing to work for the betterment of the people and never be distracted by anyone, not even a handsome face or a nice package ever again.

To her surprise, the king, although he was still hurt, saw the sincerity in her eyes. He forgave her. He took her to see the Council of Elders who were having to hear about the poverty and disappointments of all the people of the kingdom. Not only that, but the people also wanted her back because they were suffering so much and had lack whereas they had known prosperity with her as Queen. The Snake had died and Asabe's beauty spell over Nyakara was broken so she became the lovely image of herself again.

The Council of Elders forgave her but also apologized because before he died, Kofi had written a confession letter that he made up the treason story against Nyakara. This was just as Sadie has told Nyakara. Kofi had wanted to come clean so he could start his life with Asabe and had finally arranged a date with her for that night. The elders and the king all agreed to reinstate her right to the Throne. The king had not divorced her, so he reversed her exile from the palace, and they reunited.

Together, they worked to rebuild their relationship and kingdom. The king began to pay more attention to his wife and appreciate her in every way.

Given a second chance, this time, Nyakara used her wisdom not for personal gain, but to guide others, sharing the lessons she had learned through her fall from grace.

When Sadie told Nyakara that the Snake would die, she didn't know that Tumo would also die. Nyakara didn't realize how close that Snake and Tumo were. She mourned Tumo at the same time King Jahlani re-mourned the loss of his wife now that he knew how she died. But then they both began to concentrate on one another and kingdom business. Queen Nyakara got so much attention that she became pregnant very soon after reuniting with King Jahlani.

Sadie was invited to become the kingdom's spiritual advisor and personal advisor now that Kofi was gone. One day in a hallway in the palace Sadie and Queen Nyakara whispered, " "No, Tumo was saving your life; he really loved you."

"What! He really loved me?"

"Well, yes, his version of love."

"Why didn't he want to see me when I went to him? I tried to seduce him, and it didn't even work."

"He was saving your life."

"How so?"

"The Snake was looking for you to kill you."

Nyakara gasped!

"Tumo hid you. Tumo was the point of contact for the Snake to reach you, that's why he couldn't be with you that night. That's why he sent you to another house and stayed far away from you."

"He was so evil toward me, rude and demeaning."

"He was trying to get you out of harm's way. He was trying to get you away from the Snake."

Nyakara was shocked. She had not known how close the Snake had come to taking her life. Oh my! I didn't know. But somehow settled knowing that he really did love her and did something so valiant that may have cost him his own life.

Prosperity Returns

The kingdom flourished once again, but this time, the people saw a different queen. A queen who understood the fragility of power, the importance of loyalty, and the value of humility. Queen Nyakara had learned the hard way that power, when abused, can destroy everything. But power, when used with compassion and integrity, can heal even the deepest wounds. Nyakara fulfilled her own words--, she really was a healer now. First, she had to be healed herself, then she could help heal others in a lasting way.

And so, Nyakara's story became a legend, a tale told to remind all who seek power that it is not enough to rise to the top. True greatness lies in how we handle our fall and how we rise again, stronger and wiser.

Lessons

In today's society, the story of Queen Nyakara teaches us a powerful lesson: power is fleeting, and those who seek it without responsibility risk losing everything. How it may be lost is devised in the evil minds of evil people, even those who look like regular people, or those who are so beautiful and perfect, but are really angels of light.

Those who are in power must be wise and discerning because every pretty or handsome face that comes along is not always honest and can have hidden motives.

Those who follow leaders – any leaders, must be sure of their leader's source of strength and power by knowing who or what they worship. If not, instead of those leaders helping you, they could be looking in your direction to take from you or hurt you. They won't say that they will turn on the smiles and the charm to get what they want from you.

A true leader needs to also be spiritually wise and not let him or herself be led away into flights of fancy, pleasure or the lust of this world, because what they do will affect everyone that they are leading.

The End

For more tales of power, betrayal, and redemption read other books by Nia Zola and also tune in to her channel on You Tube, Africa Untold Tales.

You may view the abbreviated You Tube video version of this story on the Africa Untold Tales channel. It is entitled: ***JANGO: The Scent of Trouble.***
https://www.youtube.com/watch?v=NMRlqv1 8_uM

There are other fine stories on that channel as well.
https://www.youtube.com/@AfricaUntold-llc

There are other fine stories on that channel as well.
https://www.youtube.com/@AfricaUntold-11c